I0783552

Need Love
Written by Catherine Valleroy
Illustrated by Tera Colleen

I dedicate this book to
Noel who needed love
and Dave who gave it.

One day a little child got very dismayed!

So many things out of their control,
they became quite afraid!

To their loved one they did run,
Arms stretched upward for a hug...

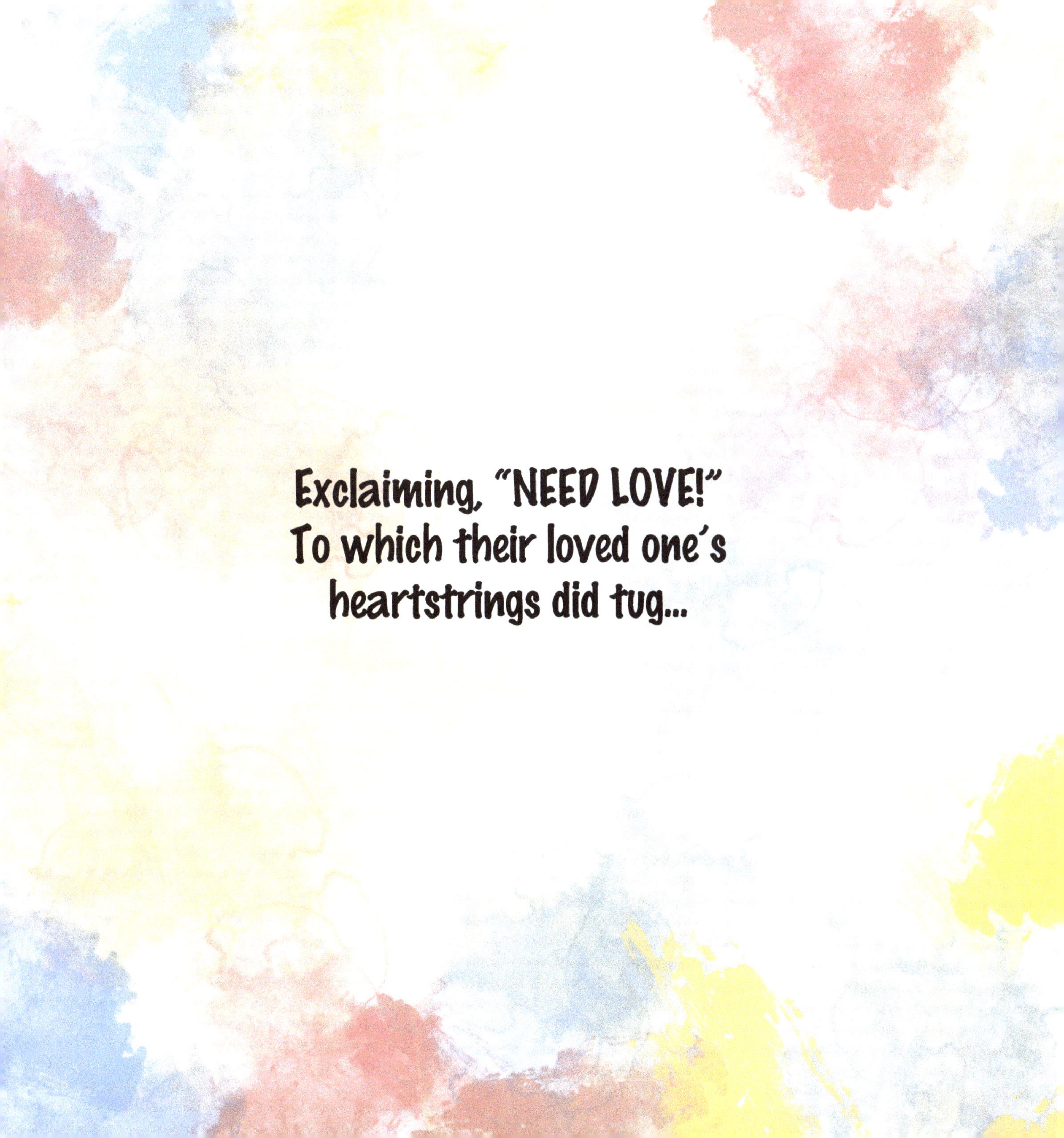

Exclaiming, "NEED LOVE!"
To which their loved one's
heartstrings did tug...

So the loved one scooped up the child and
loved them straight away.
And the little child was so comforted,
they began to feel okay.

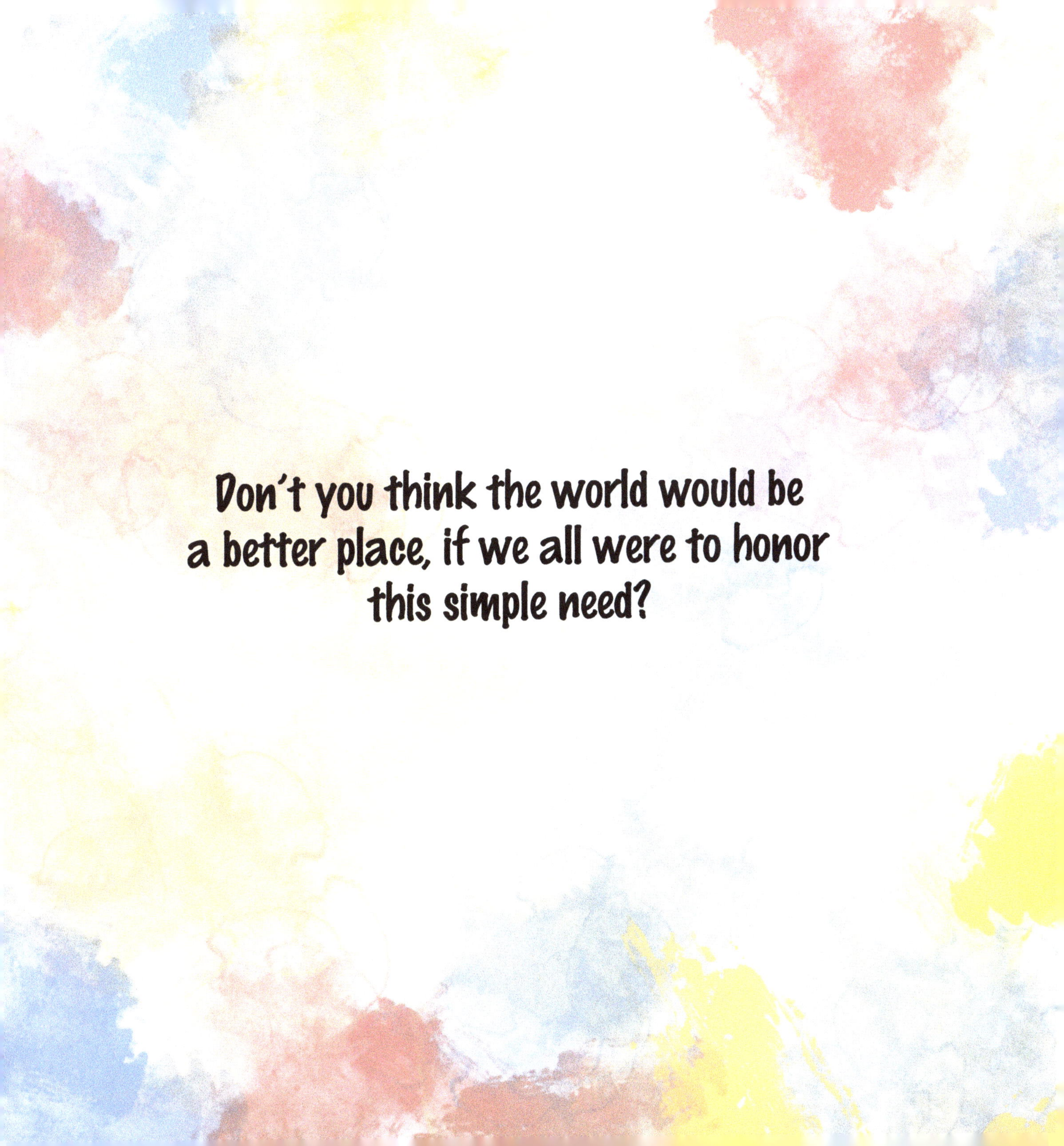
Don't you think the world would be
a better place, if we all were to honor
this simple need?

For needing and giving love
are important acts indeed.

So, don't be stingy or selfish
with this offering you make.

Love

For not putting love out into the world
is a very big mistake!

So next time you need love,
ask for it with all your might!

Need Love!

For the acts of needing and
giving love can make all things
all right!

The Beginning...